Best Stories for
Five-Year-Olds

Best Stories for Five-Year-Olds
First Published by Bloomsbury Publishing Plc in 1997
38 Soho Square, London W1V 5DF

Enid Blyton

Copyright © Text Enid Blyton Limited
Copyright © Illustrations Guy Parker-Rees 1997

The moral right of the author and illustrator has been asserted
A CIP catalogue record of this book is available from the
British Library

ISBN 0 7475 3225 7

Printed in England by Clays Ltd, St Ives plc

10 9 8 7 6 5 4 3 2 1

Cover design Mandy Sherliker

Best Stories for Five-Year-Olds

Enid Blyton
Pictures by Guy Parker-Rees

Bloomsbury

Enid Blyton titles available at Bloomsbury
Children's Books

Adventure!
Mischief at St Rollo's
The Children of Kidillin
The Secret of Cliff Castle
Smuggler Ben
The Boy Who Wanted a Dog
The Adventure of the Secret Necklace

Happy Days!
The Adventures of Mr Pink-Whistle
Run-About's Holiday
Bimbo and Topsy
Hello Mr Twiddle
Shuffle the Shoemaker
Mr Meddle's Mischief
Snowball the Pony
The Adventures of Binkle and Flip

Enid Blyton Age-Ranged Story Collections
Best Stories for Six-Year-Olds
Best Stories for Seven-Year-Olds
Best Stories for Eight-Year-Olds

Contents

Dear Children

I am Enid Blyton's daughter and when I was a little girl she used to read to me every night before I went to bed. The stories were not in a book full of pictures like this, but typed on paper because she had written them that day.

I sat on my mother's knee with our two dogs lying beside us and a cat on a chair nearby. Bimbo the cat was a cream Siamese, Sandy was a brown and white terrier and Bobs was black and white. When you read the story 'Sandy and the Moon', try to imagine the little brown and white puppy and Bobs, the black and white terrier. I used to help look after them and I loved putting the clean straw into their kennel. Bobs was my mother's favourite dog and she taught him to do all sorts of clever tricks.

I do hope that you will enjoy these stories.

With love from

Gillian

Please Shut the Gate

'There's a dear little baby kid at the farm,' said Mother to Ted and Tessie, just as they were about to set off to school one morning.

'A tiny little goat!' said Tessie. 'Oh, I would so like to see it. Ted, let's hurry, then we can ask the farmer's wife if we can go and see the little kid.'

'Now have you both got your satchels?' called Mother. 'Is your mid-morning lunch in them? Have you got your homework with you, and your pencils and rulers?'

'Yes, we've got everything!' called back the twins and ran off in a hurry. They came to the farm and saw Mrs Straw feeding her hens.

'Please may we see the baby kid?' asked Tessie.

'Of course,' said Mrs Straw. 'It's in the little field, there, with its mother. But please shut the gate, dears – I don't want the nanny goat let out.'

The children ran off to the little field. They put down their satchels on the grass and opened the gate between them, because it was rather stiff. Then they saw the little kid, and cried out in delight.

'Oh, it's like a toy one! It's simply sweet. Oh, if only it belonged to us!'

The kid was tame and friendly. The children spent five minutes playing with it and then said goodbye and ran out of the field to collect their satchels again.

Then they saw a dreadful sight. The nanny goat had gone out of the gate and was standing over their satchels. She had eaten all their biscuits. She had also eaten Ted's number book and Tessie's writing book. She had even eaten Ted's rubber! And she was just about to chew up his best pencil when he shooed her off.

Tessie ran crying to Mrs Straw. 'That horrid nanny goat came out and ate our biscuits! She's eaten some of our books.'

'Miss Brown will be very cross,' said Ted. 'Will you smack that goat hard, Mrs Straw? Now we shall have to buy new pencils and books and we have no biscuits for lunch.'

'Now how did she get out of the field to eat all that?' asked Mrs Straw. 'Who could have been silly enough to leave the gate open? For otherwise she could not have got out.'

Oh, dear – the two children went very red and didn't say another word. Who left the gate open? Why, they did, of course.

The Wind and the Sun

Once upon a time the Wind and the Sun had a quarrel.

'I am far stronger than you,' boasted the Wind. 'I can tear down chimneys, pull up trees and send ships scudding before me. You can do none of these things.'

'Yet I am stronger than you,' said the Sun. 'You are foolish, Wind, to quarrel like this.'

'Very well,' said the Wind, 'we will have a trial of strength to prove which of us is the stronger. What shall we do?'

'Do you see that traveller down there?' said the Sun. 'He wears a red cloak round his shoulders. Shall we say that whichever of us can get his cloak off first is the stronger of the two?'

'Agreed!' cried the Wind. 'I will try first, and I tell you I shall certainly win!'

The Wind began. First of all he blew very hard round the traveller. He took hold of the man's cloak and pulled at it. He jerked it this way and that. The traveller was afraid it would be blown off, so he tied it more tightly and held it close round his neck, for he was cold.

The Wind blew more strongly still. He called upon the rain, and drenched the man through from top to toe. The traveller shook the drops from himself, pulled his cloak more tightly round him, and went on his way, complaining bitterly.

The Wind grew angry. He blew up a hurricane and spun the man forward, trying to rip his cloak from him. He howled in his ear. He roared for hail to come, and soon the poor man was trying to protect his head from the stinging balls of ice. He was so cold that he wished he had ten cloaks. He took off the belt from his coat and buckled it tightly round his cloak so that it could not possibly be blown away.

The Wind was defeated, and called mockingly upon the Sun to try *his* power.

The Sun shone out and the clouds and mist fled away. The wind was quiet, the rain stopped. The Sun shone very steadily, and his rays began to dry the traveller's wet cloak.

The man unbuckled his belt and let his cloak hang free from his shoulders, so that it might dry easily. Still the Sun shone down with a steady heat. Soon the traveller felt warm, and unbuttoned his cloak at the neck.

The Sun went on shining. The man began to puff and blow, for he grew hot. He fanned himself with his handkerchief, and took off his hat. The Sun shone and shone.

And suddenly, to the Wind's dismay, and the Sun's delight, the traveller threw off his heavy cloak, and went striding on his way without it. He could not bear the heat of it any longer!

'Gently does it!' cried the Sun to the Wind. 'I've won! Roaring and blustering are never much good, you know! Gently does it!'

Wizard Ho-Ho's Hen

One day Bobbo, the pixie, passed by the cottage of the Wizard Ho-ho, and what should he see him doing but stroking a fine chocolate-coloured hen. At the same time he said:

'Lay me an egg, my dear little hen,
An egg made of chocolate,
While I count ten!'

The Wizard then counted ten very slowly, and at the end of his counting the hen cackled loudly. The Wizard picked up a chocolate egg that she had laid for him, all complete with a

bright red ribbon round it! He placed
it on a dish, and said:

'My dear little egg, you're rather
    wee,
Please grow a bit larger while I
    count three!'

He counted three, and to Bobbo's
enormous surprise the egg grew three
times as large!

'Ooh!' said Bobbo, running off in a
hurry as the Wizard looked round
and saw him. 'Ooh! What a fine hen
to have at Easter! Fancy laying
chocolate eggs like that!'

Now the more Bobbo thought
about it, the more he wished he could
borrow that hen – and then he
suddenly saw the brown bird wander-
ing about all by itself.

So he caught the hen and took it
into his kitchen. He stroked it, and
said:

'Lay me an egg, my dear little hen,
An egg made of chocolate,
While I count ten!'

Then he counted ten, and the hen
cackled loudly and laid him an egg
made of chocolate, this time with a
blue ribbon round it. Bobbo was
delighted. He picked it up, put it on a
dish, and said:

'My dear little egg, you're rather
    wee,
Please grow a bit larger while I
    count three!'

The egg began to grow whilst Bobbo counted three – but when he had finished counting, the egg still went on growing. Bobbo was very much surprised, and at first he was pleased, because he thought the bigger the egg, the more chocolate there would be to eat. But, oh, dear me! That egg didn't know when to stop. It grew as big as the table, which broke beneath its weight. Then it grew right up to the ceiling, and pushed its way through into Bobbo's bedroom above!

The pixie was frightened. He cried out to the egg to stop, but it took no notice.

'It will push the roof off my house!' wept Bobbo. 'Oh, I must go and beg the Ho-ho Wizard to help me!'

He rushed off and told the Ho-ho Wizard what had happened.

'Ho, ho!' he said. 'You are being well punished, Bobbo. You are very naughty. If you had brought my hen

back to me when you found it loose,
I would have given you a beautiful
Easter egg. Now you have got one
that you don't want. Ho, ho!'

After a while he went back with
Bobbo, and said to the egg:

'My dear little egg, you're rather
   tall,
I think I prefer you to be quite
   small!'

The egg at once shrunk until it was
very tiny indeed. The Wizard put it
into his pocket, picked up the hen,
said goodbye to Bobbo, and went

home. The pixie was left with his ceiling and kitchen table to mend, and he was very sad indeed.

Sandy and the Moon

O ne bright night Sandy, the puppy, saw the moon sailing in the sky, and it frightened him.

'What's that?' he asked Bobs, the dog.

'The moon,' said Bobs. 'Can you see him looking at you? There's a man in the moon, you know, Sandy. Be careful that he doesn't eat you!'

'He'd better be careful I don't eat him!' said Sandy, fiercely. 'Ho, Moon? Do you see my sharp teeth? Be careful, or I will eat you!'

The moon took no notice at all, but went on sailing swiftly through the clouds. Every time it came out from behind them Sandy thought that the moon was staring at him, and he grew very angry.

'Go away!' he barked. 'You staring moon, how dare you look at me like that?'

He barked and barked, he growled in his throat, and he snarled and snapped – but still the moon sailed in the sky and was as bright as ever. At last Sandy's neck ached with looking upwards, and he went into his kennel to lie down.

He hadn't been there very long before his mistress came down the path and whistled softly. 'Ho, Bobs, ho, Sandy? What about a walk on this lovely night?'

Out rushed both the dogs and danced round their mistress. Then down the lane they went, barking and jumping. Sandy had forgotten all about the moon – until suddenly he came to a large puddle. And there, shining in the middle of it, was the silver moon! It looked up at Sandy and it seemed to laugh at him. 'Here I am again!' it said.

'Ha!' wuffed Sandy, in excitement. 'You've got into that puddle, have you! All right! I'll have you now!'

He scraped and scraped at the puddle to get the moon, but he couldn't get it. It broke up into little bits, but it joined itself together again in a few moments, and laughed at Sandy.

'I'll get you somehow!' growled Sandy. 'I know! I'll drink the puddle, and find you at the bottom of it. Then I'll chew you into bits!'

So he began to drink the puddle. It was a large one, but Sandy wouldn't give up. He drank and drank, and his little body swelled up like a balloon. At last he had drunk it all up, and he looked for the moon at the bottom – but it wasn't there!

Just then his mistress came back with Bobs, and she looked at him in surprise. 'Whatever have you drunk all that puddle for?' she asked. 'You must have been thirsty, Sandy.'

'The moon was in there,' said Sandy, 'so I drank the water to get at it – but oh, Mistress, the moon isn't there now, so I must have drunk it!

Oh, it's giving me such a pain! Oh, I've got the moon inside me!'

Then Bobs laughed till his tail nearly fell off. 'Look up into the sky!' he said, and Sandy looked. There was the moon, sailing quietly between the clouds. 'Well, however did it get back there?' cried Sandy in amazement – and he doesn't know to this very day!

The Birthday Cake

Once upon a time Pom-Pom the Pixie found eleven eggs hidden in one corner of his barn. He hadn't kept hens for some time, so he knew they must be very old eggs. He was a mean person, and a horrid idea came into his head.

'I'll send them to the Bee Woman,' he thought. 'She'll think I have made her a lovely present, and perhaps she'll give me some of her new honey.'

So he put them into a basket and sent them to the Bee Woman.

'Dear, dear!' she said, when she had got them. 'Now I really don't want any more eggs today, I've just bought twelve. I know! I'll send them to the Balloon Man! He's been ill, and will be glad of them!'

So she sent them across to the Balloon Man. When he saw them, he sighed.

'Now, what a pity!' he said. 'This is
the third lot of eggs I have had sent
me today! Well, well, I shall never be
able to eat them all, that's certain – so
I'll send them to my poor old Aunt
Toppytoes. I'm sure she'll be very
glad of them, indeed.'

So he sent them to his Aunt
Toppytoes, and she was so surprised
to get a present.

'But, oh, it's eggs!' she said. 'And
the doctor says I mustn't eat a single
egg for a month. So I'd better think
of some one to send them to. I know!
I'll send them to Chippy the Elf. He's
fond of making cakes, and these will

come in handy for his baking day!'

So the eggs were sent to Chippy. He was delighted with them. 'I'll make a fine birthday cake for Pom-Pom!' he decided. 'It's his birthday tomorrow, and it will be a lovely present for him. He's having a party, so it will come in very useful.'

Now Chippy had got a cold, so he didn't smell how bad the eggs were when he broke them and beat them into his flour.

He made a beautiful cake, and iced it all over, and then wrote 'A happy birthday' on it. When Pom-Pom saw it he was very joyful.

'It shall be for my party!' he said. 'Thank you very much, Chippy.'

But, oh, dear! What a dreadful cake that was when it came to be eaten. Everybody made a face and choked terribly.

'You made it of bad eggs,' said Pom-Pom to Chippy, in a very cross voice.

'I got the eggs from Mrs Toppytoes,' said Chippy. 'Were they bad, Mrs Toppytoes?'

'I don't know,' said Aunt Toppytoes. 'I got them from the Balloon Man. Were they bad, Balloon Man?'

'I don't know,' said the Balloon Man. 'I got them from the Bee Woman. Were they bad, Bee Woman?'

'I don't know,' she said. 'I got them from Pom-Pom himself. If they were bad, he has spoilt his own birthday cake, and it serves him right!'

And I think it did, don't you?

The Chocolate Rabbit

In Mother Buttercup's shop there were lots of Easter eggs, marzipan chickens and chocolate rabbits. In the middle of the window sat the biggest rabbit of all. He was very fine indeed, and was made of chocolate from his tail to his long ears.

He was a very proud rabbit, and thought he was meant for great things. All the children who came by admired him, and that made him vainer than ever – so you can guess what a shock it was for him when the yellow chicken next to him told him that he was made to be eaten!

'*Eaten*!' said the rabbit in horror. '*Eaten*! I never heard of such a thing! Why, I mean to be king of the rabbits before the year is out!'

Now just at that minute a little girl came into the shop to buy him. Mother Buttercup lifted him out of the window and popped him into a paper bag – but the rabbit nibbled a hole in it, leapt to the floor, and was out of the door in a twinkling!

'Come back, come back!' shouted the little girl. 'I want you!'

But the rabbit didn't stop. Not he! *He* wasn't going to be eaten! He raced down the street, and ran between the legs of a big brown dog.

'Come back, come back!' shouted the dog, sniffing the smell of chocolate. 'I want you!'

But the rabbit didn't stop. Not he! *He* wasn't going to be eaten! He ran round the corner, jumped over a wall, and landed right on top of a Persian cat, who was asleep in the sun. The cat woke up with a jump, and as soon as she saw that the rabbit was made of chocolate, she shouted after him.

'Come back! Come back! I want you!'

But the rabbit didn't stop. Not he! *He* wasn't going to be eaten. He ran straight on, and suddenly, splash! he fell into a pond. He struggled out, dripping wet, and oh, how cold he felt! He began to shiver and shake, and longed to get warm.

Very soon he came to where a group of children were making a picnic fire in a wood. The rabbit crept close up to the flames and sat down to warm himself.

'Who are you, little rabbit?' asked the children in surprise.

'I'm a chocolate rabbit, but I'm *not* going to be eaten!' said the rabbit, fiercely. 'Don't come near me! I fell into a pond, and now I want to get

warm. If you come near me, I'll bite you!'

'Let's go and find Mother and tell her about this funny rabbit,' said the children, half afraid to go near. So they went to find their mother. The rabbit crept nearer and nearer to the fire. Suddenly he began to feel sleepy. His head drooped forward and his eyes closed.

'I *won't* be eaten! I *won't* be eaten!' he said dreamily – and that was the last he said – for suddenly the heat of the fire melted him, and in a moment there was no rabbit left, only a pool of brown chocolate on the ground.

And when the children came back with their mother, what did they see? Nothing but a big brown dog and a Persian cat licking something by the fire!

A Little Snow House

The snow was deep on the ground. Pip and Jinky had built two snowmen, and thrown snowballs at one another till they were tired.

They thought they would build a snow house for themselves. 'You know, it's warmer under the snow than on top,' Pip told Jinky. 'So if we build a house under the snow, we shall be as warm as if we have blankets on. Aunt Twinkle told me that last week.'

'Ooooh yes, let's build a snow

house then,' said Jinky. 'I'd love that.'

So they began to build a snow house. They burrowed deep in a snowdrift, and made a big hole there. Then they began to build a nice house of snow. They made the walls, and patted the snow down as they built them.

'Now we'll put on the roof,' said Jinky. 'We'll make it nice and round. It will be easier to build that way.'

'We'll make holes in the walls for windows,' said Pip. 'But not very big ones, because we don't want the cold air to come in. And we'll make a little door too. Isn't this fun, Jinky?'

They worked very hard, and when teatime came the house was quite finished. The two pixies looked at it proudly. They were hot with their work, and the little snow house seemed cosy and snug.

'Let's live here!' said Pip. 'Let's fetch our beds in and sleep here. We shall be as warm as toast.'

'Well, the house will only take one bed,' said Jinky. 'I'll get mine. We can cuddle up together.'

They put the bed in the snow house. Then they sat on it, eating the jam sandwiches that Aunt Twinkle had given them. 'It's a bit cold after all,' said Pip with a sudden shiver. 'Let's make a little fireplace, and put some twigs there for a fire. That will be very snug. Then we'll curl up in bed and go to sleep.'

So they made a cheerful fire, curled up in bed and fell asleep. But alas, they soon woke up, and felt a cold drip-drip falling down on them. The house was vanishing fast! They were wet through.

'Oh, what's happened?' cried Pip. 'Jinky, quick. What has happened to our little house?'

Well, you know what had happened, don't you? Funny old Pip and Jinky! It wasn't very clever to build a fire in a snow house, was it?

Cluck-cluck!
Cluck-cluck!

'What's that noise?' wondered James, as he walked down the lane, wheeling his barrow. He was looking for some dandelion leaves to take to his pet rabbit. 'It's a noise like a hen makes – cluck-cluck-cluck!'

He put down his barrow and went towards the noise. Yes – it was a hen. It was in the hedge and was caught in some barbed wire, poor thing.

'Cluck – cluck!' it said. 'Cluck-cluck-cluck!'

'Oh – your leg is all torn with the

wire!' said James. 'Keep still, hen, and I'll try and get you out without letting the wire hurt you any more!'

The hen kept still, liking this little boy with the kind voice. James worked away at the wire, and got the leg free. He scratched his hand rather badly, but he didn't bother about that. The hen must be freed before it hurt its other leg!

'There!' he said at last. 'You're free.

Can you walk, hen, or is your leg too bad?'

The hen tried to walk, but its hurt leg was too painful, and it sat down in the lane with a sad little cluck.

'Poor thing!' said James. 'Look – I'll lift you into my barrow and take you down to the farm. I expect the farmer's wife will know how to mend your poor leg.'

The hen let him lift her into his barrow. She sat on top of the dandelion leaves and clucked loudly.

'You're saying "Thank you," aren't you?' said James. 'I'm glad I found you. Well, we'll soon be at the farm.'

He wheeled his barrow carefully all the way to the farm. He went to the farmhouse and knocked at the door. Mrs Straw, the farmer's wife, opened it.

She was very surprised to see James with the barrow and hen.

'Your hen got caught on some barbed wire and its leg is hurt,' said James. 'Can you lift her out, Mrs

Straw? She's rather heavy.'

'Bless you – you're a kind little soul!' said Mrs Straw, and lifted the hen out gently. 'Oh, her poor leg – never mind, I can soon put that right.'

'Oh look!' said James suddenly. 'There's an egg in my barrow! Oh, Mrs Straw, the hen must have laid it there. It's lovely and warm – feel! Where shall I put it?'

'Back in your barrow!' said Mrs Straw. 'That's the hen's way of

returning your kindness, James. She laid the egg for you, not for me. You take it home and have it for your breakfast!'

'Oh thank you!' said James, in delight. 'I've never had an egg specially laid for me before! What a nice hen!'

Well, he had it for his breakfast – and it was the nicest one he has ever tasted! He's going to the farm to find out how the hen's leg is today, so maybe she will have laid him a second egg – you never know!

The Complaining
Tadpole

There was once a tadpole who thought he knew everything. He took no notice of what the bigger tadpoles told him, and when a grown frog said he was very silly to go so near the ducks on the pond he was angry.

'Pooh!' he said, rudely. 'What do you know about ducks, I should like to know! Why, I've been told that you've only been in this pond for five weeks, so you may be sure I shan't listen to you! I've been in the pond all my life!'

'Well, you're only three weeks old!' said the frog. 'Don't be silly. You want telling off. Hi, all you frogs, here is a tadpole that wants smacking!'

'So all the frogs swam up, and the cheeky tadpole was told off. He was so angry! He swam off to the other tadpoles and told them all about it.

'What use are frogs!' he cried. 'Nasty, ill-natured things! Down with frogs! I shall go round and complain about them to everything in the pond.'

So he swam off alone, and went to where a minnow and a stickleback were chatting to one another.

'I want to complain about frogs!' he said. 'Down with frogs! Chase them out of the pond! Do you agree with me, stickleback and minnow?'

The fish laughed so much that they couldn't answer, and the tadpole swam away in disgust, wondering what they were laughing at. He saw a great black water beetle, and wriggled up to him.

'Down with frogs!' he said. 'Chase them out of the pond! Do you agree with me, black water beetle?'

The beetle stared at the tadpole in surprise, and then laughed till it could laugh no more, and had to rise to the top of the water to take more air in to breathe.

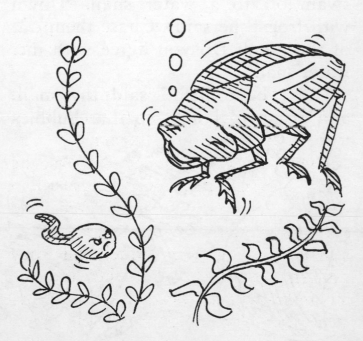

'Silly creature!' said the tadpole, and swam off to a newt. 'Down with frogs!' he said to the astonished newt. 'Chase them out of the pond! Do you agree with me, newt?'

The newt began to laugh, and swallowed a fly he was eating in such a hurry that it went down the wrong way and he began to choke.

'Stupid thing!' said the tadpole, and swam off to a water snail. 'Down with frogs!' he said. 'Chase them out of the pond! Do you agree with me, water snail?'

'Don't be foolish!' said the snail, and began to laugh, so that bubbles

of air escaped from his mouth and rose up to the top of the water in a silvery line.

'Why does every one laugh when I say, "Down with frogs!"?' cried the tadpole crossly. 'I don't think it's funny!'

The water snail laughed again. Then the newt, the black water beetle, the minnow and the stickleback all came up and began to laugh too.

'We'll make you a promise, tadpole,' they said. 'If you come back in six weeks' time and say, "Down with frogs! Chase them out of the pond!" we'll do it. Now go away!'

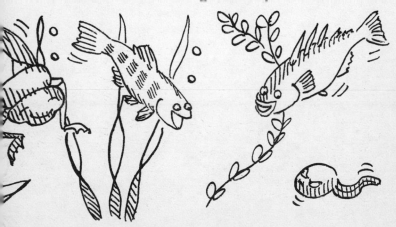

'I'll be back in six weeks' time!' promised the tadpole, eagerly, and swam off, very much delighted. But when the six weeks were up, he didn't go back! And who can tell me why?

The Fairy and the Policeman

One night a fairy wandered into the nursery, where the toys were all talking and playing together. They were delighted to see her, and begged her to tell them all about herself.

'Well, I live under the white lilac bush in the garden,' she said. 'But, you know, I'm afraid I shall soon have to move.'

'Why?' asked the toys in surprise.

'Because,' said the fairy with a shiver, 'a great fat frog has come to live there. I don't mind frogs a bit usually, but this one likes to cuddle close to me, and he is so cold and clammy! When I move away from him he gets angry. I am so afraid that he will bring his brother and sisters there too, and if they all cuddle up to me for warmth I'm sure I shall die!'

'Dear me,' said the toy policeman, in a shocked voice. 'But, you know, my dear little fairy, frogs have no right to go to the place you have made your home. That is trespassing, and isn't allowed.'

'Well, how can I prevent them?' said the fairy. 'They are much stronger than I am.'

'Look,' said the toy policeman, taking a whistle from his pocket. 'Here is a police whistle. Take it home with you to the lilac bush. If those frogs do come, blow it loudly and I will come to your help at any time, night or day.'

'Oh, thank you,' said the fairy, and she slipped the whistle into her pocket. Off she went, out of the window, waving merrily to the toys.

And the very next night, just as the toys were playing 'Here we go round the Mulberry Bush,' they heard the police whistle being blown very loudly indeed.

'The fairy is whistling for help!' cried the policeman, and he jumped out of the window. He ran to the white lilac bush, and underneath he saw such a strange sight.

There were seven yellow and green frogs, all crowding round the poor little fairy, and she was so frightened. The policeman drew his truncheon, and began to smack the frogs smartly. Smack! Smack! They squeaked and croaked in pain and began to hop away.

The fairy threw her arms round the brave policeman's neck and hugged him.

'Come back to the nursery with me,' begged the toy policeman. 'You'll be safe there. I'm afraid the frogs might come back again when you are asleep.'

So the fairy went back to the nursery with the policeman, and all the toys welcomed her. She played games with them and had a perfectly lovely time. When they were hungry they went to the little toy sweet shop and bought some peppermint rock. It was great fun!

'I do wish I could live here with you,' said the fairy, 'it's so jolly.'

'Well, why can't you?' asked the policeman. 'There's plenty of room in the toy cupboard. We can hide you right at the back.'

So that night the fairy slept in the toy cupboard with all the other toys – and what do you think? Early the next morning Gwen, the little girl who lived in the nursery, went to the cupboard and began to pull all the toys out. Oh, how the fairy trembled!

'Keep quite still and pretend you are a toy doll,' whispered the policeman. So she did.

'Oh, oh! Here's a beautiful fairy doll!' cried Gwen, suddenly seeing the fairy. 'Where did she come from? Oh, Mummy, look!'

She pulled out the doll and showed it to her mother. The fairy kept so still and made herself so stiff that she really did look just like a fairy doll.

'Isn't she beautiful?' cried the little girl. 'Where did she come from, Mummy?'

'Well, really, I don't know,' said Mummy, surprised. 'I've never seen her before. It's the nicest toy you have, Gwen.'

Gwen played with the fairy doll all day long and loved her very much. The fairy was delighted, and when night came and all the toys came alive once more, she danced round the nursery in joy.

'I shall be a toy now instead of a fairy,' she cried. 'I shall live with you in the cupboard and be happy.'

'Hurrah!' shouted the toys. 'What fun!'

The fairy is still there, and Gwen is very fond of her. Wouldn't she be surprised if she knew that her doll is really a fairy?

The Cat, the Mouse, and the Fox

Once upon a time a cat walked into a trap. Click! The catch of the cage sprang down, and the cat was caught. She mewed pitifully, and a little mouse heard her and came running.

'Press back the spring, little mouse,' begged the cat. 'Set me free, I pray you!'

'No,' said the mouse. 'You would eat me!'

'I give you my word that I would do no such thing,' said the cat. So the little mouse pressed back the spring and out from the cage leapt the cat. She pounced at once on the mouse, and the tiny creature squeaked in fright. 'You promised not to eat me if I did you a kindness.'

'You were foolish to believe me,' said the cat scornfully. The mouse squeaked again, and a fox who was running by paused and listened.

'What is the matter?' he asked. The mouse, with many squeaks, told him all that had happened. The fox winked at the mouse, put on a most innocent look, and turned to the cat.

'Let me get this tale right,' he said. 'The mouse was in the trap, Cat—'

'No,' said the cat, '*I* was in the trap.'

'Sorry,' said the fox. 'Well, *you*, Cat, were in the trap, and I came running by—'

'No, no!' cried the cat impatiently. 'The *mouse* came running by.'

'Of course,' said the fox, 'the trap was in the cat and the mouse came—'

'Stupid creature!' cried the cat angrily. 'Of course the trap was not in me! I tell you *I* was in the trap.'

'Pardon, pardon!' said the fox humbly. 'Do let me get it right. Now – you were in the mouse and the trap came running by—'

'Listen!' cried the cat in a rage. 'Have you no ears or understanding? I was in the trap and the *mouse* came running by—'

The cat almost flew at the fox, she was in such a rage at his stupidity. Her tail swung from side to side, and she spat rudely at the innocent-looking fox opposite to her.

'Who would think anyone could be

so stupid?' she hissed. 'And you are supposed to be so sharp, Fox! Never have I met anyone so slow and dense. Listen! *I* was in the trap and the *mouse* came running by. Surely that is easy to understand!'

'Quite easy,' said the fox, blinking his sharp eyes. 'I've got it this time, Cat. The trap was in the mouse and—'

The cat stared at the fox as if she could not believe her ears. Could anyone be so stupid? She spat again and then glared in a fury. 'I will *show* you what happened,' she said. 'Then perhaps you will understand at last, you very stupid fox!'

She jumped into the trap and looked out through the bars at the fox. 'See,' she said, 'I was in the trap like this, and the mouse came running by.'

'I see *now*,' said the fox, and he snapped down the spring. 'Thank you, Cat, for being so patient! The mouse will *not* set you free this time. To be ungrateful to a friend is a hateful thing – think it over in peace and quiet, for you will be a long time in the trap.'

Then, leaving the cat in the cage,

the fox and the mouse went off together. 'You will see, friend Mouse,' said the fox with a grin, 'that I am not half so stupid as I appear. Good day to you, and good luck!'

The Cuckoo Left Behind

There was once a cuckoo who wouldn't fly away when autumn came. His friends the swallows and martins were gone long since, and the cuckoos had gone too. They had flown away to warmer lands, where there were plenty of insects for the winter.

'I shall stay here,' said the cuckoo, 'the robin will help me, and so will the thrush, for they tell me that they both stay for the winter. I don't see why I should tire myself out by flying so many thousands of miles away. It is a most ridiculous idea, and very old fashioned!'

So he stayed. The autumn days were warm and bright, and the sun shone hotly down – but at night it was cold. The cuckoo found a warm spot in an ivy-covered wall, and there he roosted each night.

'How clever I am!' he said. 'There are plenty of insects about in the sunshine, and the ivy is humming day and night with them!'

The ivy was blooming then, and hosts of insects came for the nectar. The cuckoo had a fine time, for he caught many for his dinner and grew as fat as could be.

But then the frosts came. The ivy blossoms withered, and green berries came in their place. It was cold, cold, cold. The flies disappeared. No moths came. The bees were in their hives. The wasps were dead, all but the queens, and they were fast asleep in a hole underground.

The cuckoo could find nothing to
eat. He grew thin and weak, and
goodness knows what would have
happened to him if he hadn't come
one day to a tiny cottage where a
clockmaker lived. The cuckoo crept
inside for warmth and watched the
clockmaker at work.

'Let me live with you, and I will
cuckoo for you and tell you the time
when you wish to know it,' said the
cuckoo.

The clockmaker put on his spect-
acles and looked at the silly cuckoo.

Then he made a wooden clock, and built a little room at the top of it.

'See,' he said to the cuckoo. 'Creep in here. You may live there – but whenever the little hand points to an hour, you must fly out and say cuckoo! At one o'clock you must cuckoo once, and at two o'clock twice, and so on. Do you understand?'

'Yes, thank you very much,' said the cuckoo. He flew inside the clock room, and the door shut after him. There he stayed until the next hour, which was four o'clock, and then out he flew and said 'Cuckoo! cuckoo! cuckoo! cuckoo!' four times, just like that.

'Splendid!' said the clockmaker. 'I have made the first cuckoo clock in the world! What a lot of money I shall get!'

And now you know how the first cuckoo clock came to be made!

The Bear With Button Eyes

There was once a little teddy bear who had button eyes. He could see quite well with them, but he couldn't shut them to go to sleep. He didn't mind this a bit because he was always very wide awake.

Now one day, Mollie, his little mistress, took him out into the garden to play, and suddenly a dreadful thing happened. One of his button eyes came loose, and dropped into the grass! How upset the little bear was!

Mollie didn't notice it. She was setting out her tea set, and didn't see that the bear had only one eye. He did his best to show her, but she went on playing tea parties, and didn't look at him.

'Oh my, oh my!' thought the little bear, 'what am I to do? I am going to a dance with all the other toys to-night, and I can't go with only one eye!'

Then Mollie heard her mother calling her to come in and she quickly put her toys away and ran indoors, taking the teddy with her. The bear couldn't think what he was to do! He really must get his eye back before the dance that night!

He sat in the toy cupboard, very sad and quiet. His friend the bunny rabbit wondered what was the matter.

'What is making you so sad?' he asked, putting a soft paw into the teddy bear's brown one.

'One of my button eyes fell out on to the grass,' said the bear, sadly. 'Mollie didn't notice, and I am sure I don't know how I can go to a dance with only one eye. What am I to do?'

The bunny thought hard. Then he squeezed the bear's paw.

'As soon as it is night and the moon is up, I will take all the toy soldiers into the garden and they shall look for your button eye,' he said.

'Oh, thank you,' said the bear, very gratefully.

So as soon as Mollie had gone to bed, and the moon was up, the bunny rabbit made all the toy soldiers march out of their fortress and follow him into the garden. Then they looked and looked and looked for the button eye.

But they couldn't find it! It was most surprising. It wasn't anywhere in the garden at all.

A little brownie came running by, and he stopped in astonishment to see so many toy soldiers about.

'Whatever are you doing here?' he asked.

'Looking for Teddy bear's button

eye,' said the rabbit. 'He dropped it here this afternoon, and he says he can't go to our dance tonight without it.'

'Good gracious!' said the brownie. 'I know what has happened to it!'

'What?' asked all the soldiers and the bunny together.

'Why, Fairy Littlefeet came by this evening,' said the brownie, 'and she had lost a black button from her right

shoe. Suddenly she saw one in the grass, and she picked it up and sewed it on to her shoe. I lent her a needle and thread myself.'

'Oh my!' said the bunny in dismay. 'Now what are we to do? Do you know where Littlefeet lives?'

'No,' said the brownie. 'I don't. I'm afraid the bear won't get his button eye back now.'

Everyone was quite quiet, thinking what to do. Then at last the brownie spoke.

'If only you could get another button from somewhere, I could perhaps sew it on for you myself,' he said.

The bunny thanked him very much.

'There may be one in Mollie's work-basket,' he said. 'I'll go and see.'

So he and all the soldiers went back into the playroom again and hunted in Mollie's workbasket. But there were only pearl buttons there, and those wouldn't do for eyes. The bunny was in despair. What could he do for the teddy bear? It was getting nearly time to start the dance, and he did so badly want his friend to go.

Then he thought of a splendid idea. He knew that Mollie wore shoes with buttons on. If only he could find those, perhaps he could cut one off, and that would do splendidly for the bear.

So he hurried to the boot cupboard. But Mollie's black shoes had gone to be mended, and there was only a white pair there, with white buttons on.

'Perhaps a white button would do just as well,' thought the bunny. 'I expect he could see with it all right.'

So he took a pair of scissors and snipped the button from one shoe. Then he ran to the bear.

'Come along,' he said. 'I've got a button that will do for you. It's white, but I'm sure it won't matter.'

He took him to the brownie, and the little man fetched a reel of spider

thread and a pine needle. In a trice he had sewn on the white boot button, and the teddy bear had two eyes!

'I can see beautifully!' he said, looking all round. 'That is splendid! Do I look very funny?'

He did look a bit odd with one white eye and one black one, but the bunny told him that he looked lovely. So off he went to the dance feeling very happy.

Now in the morning Mollie went to put her white shoes on – and wasn't she surprised to find the button gone!

'Why, both buttons were there when I put them away yesterday,' she said. 'Where can the other one be?'

Then she suddenly caught sight of the teddy bear, staring at her with his one black button eye and his one white one. She ran to him and picked him up.

'Oh, you poor darling!' she cried. 'How did you get that white button for an eye? You had two black ones yesterday! The fairies must have

come in the night and sewn it on for you!'

Mollie looked at it carefully and saw that it was most beautifully sewn on with spider thread instead of cotton. Then she knew for certain that some fairy had been at work, and she was filled with delight.

'Now I know there are fairies!' she cried. 'Oh, Teddy, you shall keep your white eye to remind me. I do wish you could tell me what had happened!'

But he never did tell her. He still has one white and one black button for eyes, so if ever you meet him you are sure to know him!

The Nice Juicy Carrot

In the field at the back of the farm lived three grey donkeys. They were called Neddy, Biddy, and Hee-Haw. Sometimes the farmer put one into the harness belonging to a small carriage, and his little daughter drove out for a ride. But usually the donkeys didn't have much to do, and they very often quarrelled.

One day Neddy found a large juicy carrot in the ditch, and he was most excited about it. In fact, he was so excited that instead of keeping quiet about it and nibbling it till it was gone, he raised his head and cried: 'Eeyore! Eeyore! Eeyore!'

Just like that.

Well, of course, the other two donkeys came running up to see what was the matter, and they saw the nice juicy carrot too. And they wanted to eat it.

But Neddy put his thick little body in the way and said: 'No, that's my carrot.'

Biddy tried to scrape the carrot near her with her foot.

'It's *my* carrot!' she said.

'I'm the hungriest, so it's *my* carrot!' said Hee-Haw, and he tried to push the others away.

Then Neddy saw that he would not be allowed to eat it in peace, and he thought of a plan to decide which donkey should have the carrot. 'Let us see who can bray the loudest,' he said.

So they began. First Neddy brayed.

'Eeyore, eeyore, eeyore!' he cried,

and a little sandy rabbit running not far off was so astonished at the loud noise that he came near to see what it was all about.

Then Biddy brayed. 'EEYORE, EEYORE, EEYORE!' she cried, and the watching rabbit thought it a very ugly noise.

Then Hee-Haw brayed, and dear
me, his voice was so loud that a
hedgehog not far off was frightened
almost out of his life, and curled himself up into a tight ball.

'EEYORE, EEYORE, EEYORE!'
roared Hee-Haw. The listening rabbit
thought that donkeys had terrible
voices. Then, dear me, the rabbit
caught sight of that nice juicy carrot
lying just nearby in the ditch. How
his nose woffled when he saw it!

He crept out from his hiding place
and the three donkeys saw him.

'Look! There is a rabbit!' cried Hee-
Haw. 'He shall tell us which brayed
the loudest just now. Then we shall

know who wins the carrot!'

So they called to the rabbit to judge between them. But the bunny was very artful. He didn't want to see the carrot eaten by a donkey. So he looked wisely at the three grey animals and shook his head.

'There wasn't much to choose between your braying,' he said. 'Why don't you have a race? Then you could easily tell who should have the carrot.'

'That's a good idea,' said the donkeys. 'Where shall we race to, rabbit?'

'Oh, all round the field and back again to where I sit,' answered the wily rabbit. 'Now, are you ready? One, two, three, off!'

Away went the three donkeys at top speed. Round the field they went at a gallop, much to the astonishment of the farmer's wife. They panted and puffed, kicking up their heels in fine style, each trying to get ahead of the other.

They all arrived back at the starting place at the same moment. But each donkey thought it had won.

'I've won!' said Neddy.

'No, I'm first!' brayed Biddy.

'The carrot's mine!' roared Hee-Haw.

'Let's ask the rabbit who's won,' said Neddy. 'He'll know.'

So they called to the rabbit – but there was no answer. They called again, and still they had no reply. Then they looked for the carrot.

It was gone!

Umbrellas for the Dolls

Once Aunt Twinkle asked the dolls' house dolls out to tea with her and her nephews, Pip and Jinky. She liked them very much, for they were small and dainty, and had beautiful manners.

'You and Jinky can look after them at tea time,' she said to Pip. 'And just see that your manners are as good as theirs! Remember, too, not to help yourselves to the cake until everyone else has a slice.'

'But there might not be any left then,' said Pip, in alarm.

'That's just exactly why I said you're not to help yourselves,' said his aunt. 'Visitors must always come first.'

Well, the dolls' house dolls came. They were just about as big as Pip and Jinky, and they all had on their very best clothes, and looked perfectly sweet.

It was a wonderful tea, and there was plenty of cake for everyone after all. They played games after tea, and then it was time to go home.

'Oh, dear!' said one of the little dolls in dismay. 'It's pouring with rain. Our best party dresses will be spoilt.'

'I haven't enough umbrellas for you all,' said Aunt Twinkle, worried. 'Pip – Jinky – think of something quickly!'

'Half a minute!' cried Pip, and he ran out into the rain. He went to where the primrose plants grew. He had often noticed that the rain ran off their crinkly leaves – they were as good as umbrellas, those leaves! The primroses liked them crinkled because then the rain trickled off down the crinkles, and the plant itself didn't get soaked.

Pip picked twelve leaves and ran back. 'Here you are – fine green umbrellas for each of you!' he cried. 'Look at their crinkles – the rain will run down them and you won't get a drop on your pretty clothes!'

He was right. The dolls' house dolls went home safely and arrived quite dry, each holding a primrose leaf umbrella over her head. As for Pip, he and Jinky had an extra slice of cake each – they were pleased!

The Kind Little Girl

Agood many birds lived in Mary's garden. They liked Mary. She never pulled their nests to pieces, or took their eggs. She liked listening to their songs, and she knew all their names.

The robin lived in her garden, and the stumpy little wren. The blackbird lived there, and the thrush too. Many starlings came down to bathe in Mary's pond, and sat in the trees afterwards to chatter and dry their wings.

Now it was wintertime. The days

were cold and the nights were colder still. Then one day the snow came, and the birds saw that the ground was white instead of green and brown.

There was very little food to be found. The berries had been pulled from the bushes and trees, and now there were very few. It was cold, so cold!

'I can hardly uncurl my toes from the twig when I wake up in the morning!' said one sparrow to another.

'And did you know that all the puddles are frozen hard, and the pond is made of ice too?' said a listening blackbird. 'There is nothing to drink. I am so thirsty.'

'We are hungry and thirsty and cold!' said the robin. 'We shall die. This is a terrible time for us. What shall we do?'

'There is only one thing to do,' said the freckled thrush. 'We must tell that kind little girl our troubles. Surely she

will help us!'

So what do you think they all did?
They went and sat in a row on the
fence, fluffing out their feathers to
keep themselves warm, and looking
as miserable as could be!

Mary saw them. 'Poor little crea-
tures!' she cried. 'Are you so cold and
hungry? I will look after you till this
bitter weather has gone!'

She made a bird table for them –
just a sheet of board nailed to a little
pole. On the table, she put all the
scraps her mother could spare –

crumbs, scrapings from the milk-puddings, a bone or two, and some berries she had picked and dried to give the birds in winter. She put a big enamel basin of water on the bird table, so that they might drink. Each bird took a delicious sip, and held his head back to let the water trickle down his throat. They pecked at the food hungrily, and wanted to sing a thank-you song to Mary, but they couldn't see her.

'She's making warm beds for us!' sang the thrush. 'Look – she's got flowerpots to hide in the hedge – and she's stuffed them with straw or moss. Isn't she kind?'

She was kind, wasn't she, and it's no wonder they all sing songs to her in springtime. Would you like to do all that Mary did? You can if you like!

The Clever Little Pig

O nce upon a time there was a little pink pig with a nice curly tail. He was out for a walk one day when he met Mister Wolf, who was large and grey and had a long straight tail. He stared at the little pink pig and thought how nice and fat he was.

The little pink pig was scared. He had always been told that pigs and wolves didn't mix very well, and he wondered what to do. He decided to go on without saying anything at all. But that didn't do, for the wolf walked beside him and talked hard.

'Please go away, Mister Wolf,' said the pink pig. 'I don't like you.'

'But I like *you*,' said Mister Wolf. 'I like you very much. I shall come home with you, little pink pig.'

The pink pig was most alarmed, and the curl went out of his tail. It would not do to take Mister Wolf home with him, for he had four dear little piglets there. No, it would not do at all. The little pig was most worried. He hurried along with Mister Wolf, keeping close beside him, and he wondered and wondered what to do!

And at last he thought of such a good idea. He began to smile, and the curl came back into his tail once more.

'This way!' he said to the wolf when he came to the corner. 'This way! I shall be pleased to take you to my home, Mister Wolf. Perhaps you would have dinner with me?'

'I certainly will,' said Mister Wolf. Down the hill they went, and across a field. Then up a hill again until they came to a big yellow door in the hillside with a great knocker on the front. Mister Wolf was surprised to see what a big front door the little pink pig had.

'Shall I knock?' said Mister Wolf.

'Oh no, you needn't do that,' said the pink pig. 'Just walk straight in, won't you, and don't bother about wiping your feet on the mat, Mister Wolf, or any little thing like that. Walk straight in and sit down in the most comfortable chair you can find!'

The pink pig opened the door for Mister Wolf, and Mister Wolf clattered in. He didn't bother to wipe his feet at all. He just went straight in, looked round for baby piglets, and sat down in a comfortable armchair.

Bang! The front door slammed, but no little pink pig came in to join Mister Wolf. No, the pig had shot off down the hillside and was halfway home by now. You see, that wasn't his home he had taken Mister Wolf to, it was Mister Lion's home! Ho, ho, ho!

And was Mister Lion pleased to see Mister Wolf walking in at the front door without knocking, and sitting down in his comfortable armchair, with his dirty feet making a mess on the nice hearth rug? He was not!

In fact, he was in a great rage about it, and Mister Wolf was in a great fright! If you had been there you would have seen the big front door open, and a scared wolf rolling down the hillside, smarting from a big lion-kick! And you would have noticed that there was a piece bitten off the end of his tail! Aha, Mister Wolf, the little pink pig tricked you that time!

The Snowman in Boots

'Harry, let's build a snowman who really looks alive!' said Valerie.

'We can't,' said Harry. 'They always look so odd about the feet, because they have to be made of snow right down to the bottom, or they wouldn't stand up.'

'Well, I know what we can do,' said Valerie. 'We can get Daddy's old rubber boots, the ones he never wears now because they have holes in – and we can fill them with snow, and then build the snowman on top of the big boots! It will look exactly as if he has proper legs in the boots!'

'All right,' said Harry. 'It's rather a good idea.' So they began to build a snowman. First of all, they fetched the old rubber boots – they were so big that Valerie could put both her feet inside one of them! Then they stood the boots on the snowy lawn and filled them with snow.

'There,' said Valerie, pleased. 'Our snowman has two snow-feet in the boots, and two fine fat legs.'

Then they built a nice round body on top of the boots, and put a round snow head on top. Harry made some arms down by the side of the body.

'Now we'll dress him,' said Valerie. 'I'll get Daddy's old macintosh from the shed. You fetch that torn red scarf of yours, Harry, and Grandpa's big old gloves, and I'll get the funny old check cap we used for our guy on Firework Night.'

It wasn't long before the snowman

was dressed up very well indeed. The macintosh was draped round his shoulders, and came right down to his knees, just above the boots. The scarf was tied round his rather fat throat. The gloves were pinned to the end of the macintosh sleeves, filled with snow so that they looked like hands.

And then the cap was put on his round head to give him the finishing touch. He did look fine!

'A stick, now,' said Harry, pleased. 'I'll lend him the one I had for my birthday. He'll like that.'

'And oh, Harry – let's give him a nice big nose and a pair of eyes!' cried Valerie. 'He will look real with them!'

Well, the children gave him a mouth made of twigs, and big black stones for eyes and a nice big nose. They were quite startled when they looked at him.

'Good morning, Mr Frosty-Man,' said Valerie, bowing. 'I hope you are well!'

'I almost expected him to bow back to you, and take off his cap,' said Harry, with a laugh. 'Mother! Come and see Mr Frosty-Man.'

'Who?' cried Mother, looking out of the window. 'Dear me – a visitor – who can it be?'

But it wasn't a visitor, of course – it was only the funny old snowman with his cap and scarf and coat and rubber boots!

Everyone stared at him in surprise when they came by. 'Who's that?' said short-sighted Miss Spink. 'Is that Valerie's grandpa? I really must say how-do-you-do to him.'

'No, dear, no,' said her sister. 'It's just a snowman!'

The children were quite sad to have to go to bed and say good night to the snowman. He stood there in the snowy night, looking more real than ever now that it was dark. There was just a little moon, enough to show him there.

Now, in the middle of the night, two burglars came along. They meant to break into the shed at the back of the children's house and steal the bicycles there. There were three – one belonging to Valerie, one to Harry, and one to their father.

The men crept in at a gate right at the bottom of the garden. The snowman was in the front garden, so they didn't see him. They went quietly to the shed where the bicycles were kept.

Nearby was a coal bunker, and hiding inside was Paddy-Paws, the children's cat. He awoke when he heard the men whispering, and poked his black head outside.

'Hallo! Who are these men? What are they doing in our shed?' thought Paddy-Paws. 'I must go and warn the family.'

But nobody heard him scratching at the door, so nobody came to see what was the matter. He ran round into the front garden – and there he saw the snowman.

'Ah – the snowman!' he thought. 'Perhaps he can help.' So up he went and tapped the snowman on the leg.

'Mr Frosty-Man,' he said, 'will you please come round to the back garden and frighten away two men who are there?'

The snowman was most surprised. 'I can't walk,' he said, in a cold, snowy sort of voice. 'Snowmen never can!'

'Why can't you?' said Paddy-Paws. 'You're wearing boots, and that means you've got two feet, and feet can walk, can't they? Why don't you try?'

'Well – I will,' said the snowman, thinking that Paddy-Paws might be right. So he tried to lift up one foot. But it was very, very heavy. He groaned.

'I don't know how to walk,' he said. 'My legs feel heavy.'

'Oh, do try again,' begged Paddy-Paws. 'Let me loosen the snow round your feet, Mr Frosty-Man. There – can you move them now?'

'Ah – that's better,' said the snow-man, and he managed to lift up one foot. He put it in front of him.

'Now you move the other foot,'

said the cat. 'That's right. Put it in front of the first foot. Now put the first foot in front again. Oh, you're getting on well, snowman!'

'Thank you for telling me how to walk,' said the snowman, and he went slowly and heavily over the lawn, on to the path, and up to the back gate. Paddy-Paws pushed it open for him and he went through.

He came to the bicycle shed. 'I'm going to make a terrible noise now, to frighten the men,' said the cat. 'So don't be afraid. You walk up to them as I yowl.'

Paddy-Paws yowled and howled and wailed and squealed. The snowman suddenly appeared at the door of the bicycle shed just as the men came to see what the dreadful noise was.

'Hey – who's there?' said one man, startled. 'Here, Jim, let's run. Quick!'

Mr Frosty-Man stood there, very big and very fat. The moonlight glinted on his stony eyes. He raised one arm stiffly, and pointed at the men.

'Run, Jim, run!' cried the frightened man watching. 'Oh, who is it? Oh, that dreadful noise!'

The snowman placed himself right in the doorway, and the men had to pummel him to get out. They squeezed by him at last, and raced back to the gate, leaving all the bicycles behind.

'Good old Mr Frosty-Man,' said Paddy-Paws. 'You scared them all right. Now – shall I help you back to the front lawn again?'

But poor old Frosty-Man had one of his legs caught in the shed door and he couldn't move, no matter how the cat shoved and pushed. So in the end he had to stay there.

And in the morning how astonished the two children were, when they went to get their bicycles!

'Mother! Mother, look where the snowman has walked to!' cried Valerie. 'Who put him at the door of our shed? – And Mother, look at these footsteps going up and down the garden from the gate to the shed!'

'Burglars must have come to get your bicycles, I should think,' Mother said. 'But how did the snowman come to be in the doorway of the shed? He couldn't possibly have walked there by himself. It's a mystery.'

'He must have been able to walk because we gave him boots,' said Harry. 'Didn't you, Mr Frosty-Man? Mother, he winked at me with his two eyes, I saw him! He did walk here himself, I know he did.'

Well, he did, of course – and a very good thing, too. You'd better give your next snowman some boots, too.

He might find them as useful as Mr
Frosty-Man did!

The Little
Christmas Tree

There was once a hill which was covered with fir trees. They were fine trees, tall and straight, and always dressed in green, for they did not throw down their leaves in autumn as other trees did. They were evergreens.

'We must grow as tall as we can!' whispered the firs to one another. 'Tall, tall and straight.'

'I want to be the mast of a ship, then I shall always feel the wind rocking me,' said one fir.

'I want to be a telegraph post,' said another tree. 'Then all day and night

I shall hear messages whispering along the wires!'

'I would like to be a scaffolding pole, put up when new houses are built,' said a third fir tree. 'I am so very, very tall.'

So the trees talked to one another – all but one small tree which hadn't grown at all. The winter wind had once uprooted it, and it had nearly died. The woodman had replanted it, but it had never grown. It was a tiny tree, sad because it could no longer talk to its brothers.

'They are so high above me that they would not even hear my voice,' thought the little fir tree.

It was frightened when the woodman came round. It knew that the other trees were proud to know they would be masts of ships or something grand and useful – but what use would such a tiny tree be?

'One day I shall be chopped down, and made into firewood,' said the fir to itself. 'I am no use at all!'

And one morning, sure enough, the woodman came and saw the tiny tree. He didn't chop it down, but he dug it up. The little tree was sad. 'Now, this is the end of me,' it thought.

To its great surprise it was planted in a pretty tub, which was painted bright red. And then all kinds of strange things happened to it!

The woodman's wife hung strands of gay tinsel on its boughs. She put bits of cotton wool here and there to make it look as if snow had fallen.

She took bright shining glass balls and tied them to the dark little branches.

'The tree is looking lovely already!' she said. 'How pleased the children will be!'

Then she fastened twenty small and beautifully coloured candles, red, pink, yellow, blue and green, all over the tree. She tied a pretty fairy doll

on to the top spike. She hung toys here and there. The tree was so astonished that it hardly knew what to think.

On Christmas Day, the mother gave the little tree to her children. They clapped their hands in joy.

'Mother! Mother! It's a Christmas tree! Oh, Mother, it's the loveliest tree we've ever had.'

The little fir tree was glad. It was happy to give pleasure to so many people. 'Even if I am used for firewood now, I shan't mind!' it thought.

But after Christmas, the woodman took the tree from its tub, and planted it in the garden round the cottage. 'It's just right for a Christmas tree!' he said. 'We'll have it for our Christmas tree every year!'

Wasn't that good luck for the little tree? I do hope you get one just like it for Christmas Day.